PRINCESSES CAN BE PIRATES TOO!

WRITTEN BY CHRISTI ZELLERHOFF

ILLUSTRATED BY AMY DAVIS

booktrope

Booktrope Editions
Seattle WA 2012

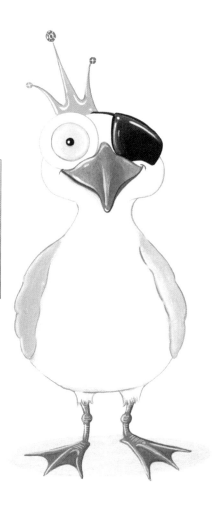

This is a work of fiction. Names, characters, places, brands, media, and incidents are either the product of the author's imagination or are used fictitiously. Any resemblance to similarly named places or to persons living or deceased is unintentional.

HARDCOVER ISBN 978-1-935961-68-0
PAPERBACK ISBN 978-1-935961-95-6

EPUB ISBN 978-1-62015-072-6

For further information regarding permissions, please contact info@booktrope.com.

Library of Congress Control Number: 2012953244

To my little princess Claire and to my pirate Henry.

-CZ

This book is dedicated to Emma and Aidan,
my biggest fans!

-AD

Only boys can be pirates?
"*Phooey!*" Says she;

A princess can be a pirate,
if she chooses to be!

A princess can do what pirates can too!

She can captain a ship and take charge of the crew.

Like pirates, she's brave,
she can sail the high seas;

She doesn't get seasick
or weak in the knees.

Though dressed in a crown and a pink fluffly dress;

She doesn't mind working
and making a mess.

Pirates aren't clean,
so why should she be?

She knows
she'll get dirty
when living at sea.

She can eat with her fingers
and slurp down her stew;

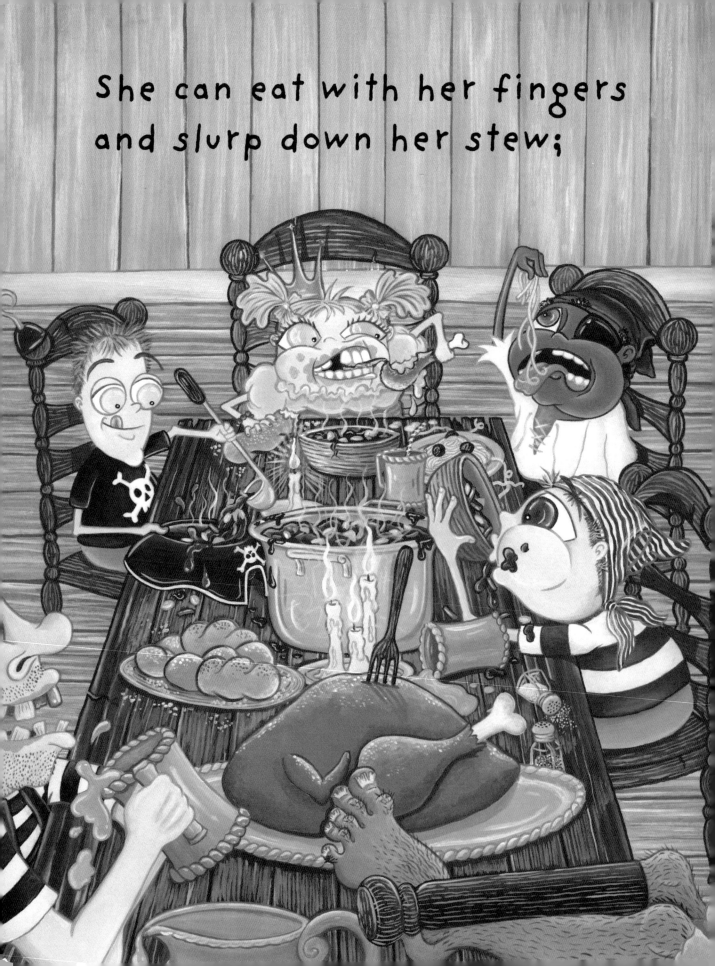

If pirates
eat messily,
a princess
can too!

A princess can work
just like strong pirates do;

She can hoist up the anchor
and swab the deck too.

She can look through a scope from up high on a mast;

She isn't afraid of a
cannon's loud blast.

Should unfriendly pirates try climbing aboard?

She can fend off the foes with a "*swoosh*" of her sword!

When the day's work is done
and the chores are all through;

She can sing and can dance
just like all pirates do.

For pirates and princesses
like the same things;

Diamonds and pearls
and red ruby rings!

Pirates don't mind getting rained on or cold;

So why should she care
when she's looking for gold!

Reading the treasure map,
looking for clues;

Pirates surround her
in hope of good news.

The treasure is marked by an "X" in the sand;

A princess can shovel
and dig with her hand.

She cheers with the pirates;
at last it's been found!

The boys keep the jewels,
but give her...the gold crown!

Only boys can be pirates?
It's simply not true!

Girls can be princesses
AND pirates too!

Made in the USA
San Bernardino, CA
02 March 2013